SPOOKY STORIES
AND OTHER SCARY STUFF

Written by Mary Packard • Illustrations by Leonid Gore

Watermill Press

Developed by Nancy Hall, Inc.
Book design by Antler & Baldwin, Inc.

Printed in Canada. Skull and flashlight made in China.

10 9 8 7 6 5 4 3 2 1

Run!

A skeleton is spooky—
A jumble of bones.
He creaks and he clatters.
He howls and he moans.

With long, bony fingers,
And holes in his face,
He waits in the graveyard
Just guarding the place.

If you should see him
Some cold, moonless night,
Then run for your life,
Or you're in for a fright.

For if he should grab you,
You might hear him say,
"I've been dying to meet you.
You really must stay!"

The Ice Skater

It was the coldest winter that anyone in Belle Harbor could remember—so cold that even the Great South Bay had frozen clear through.

One moonlit night, Heather McGillis and her friends were having the time of their lives skating on Mill Pond, which was just behind her house. Here, where no one could see them, they were all Olympic stars, gracefully gliding across the ice. Then someone would fall, sending everyone into gales of laughter. Heather's last attempt at a spin had just ended in another comical spill.

Heather was brushing herself off when she spotted a figure in the distance.

"Look!" she cried. "Over there, by the birch trees. There's someone skating. She's really good too! Let's go see who she is."

Her friends followed Heather to the other side of the pond.

As Heather introduced herself to the girl, she couldn't help but stare at the old-fashioned skates and figure-skating outfit the girl wore. "Are you from around here?" Heather asked.

"Yes, I am," said the girl. "My name is Anabelle Latham. I live at 227 Victoria Street. I go to boarding school, but I'm home for the winter solstice."

"It's nice to meet you," said Heather. "Would you like to skate with us? Maybe you could give us a few pointers."

"I'd love to," replied the girl.

They all had such fun that they skated together several times after that. Anabelle was a good skater and taught the girls how to perform several difficult spins and jumps on the ice.

But one day, when they had another skating date, Anabelle did not show up. Heather waited for her long after the others had left. She began to worry that something might have happened to her friend, so she went to Anabelle's house to make sure she was all right.

She rang the bell and an old woman opened the door. *She must be Anabelle's grandmother,* thought Heather.

"I'm Heather McGillis," she began. "Maybe Anabelle has told you about me. We've been skating together on the pond. In fact, we had a date today, but Anabelle didn't come. She's not sick, I hope."

The woman looked at Heather as if there were something wrong with her. "Why don't you come in?" she said.

Heather pointed to a yellowing photo that hung above the sofa. "That girl looks just like Anabelle," she said.

"That *is* Anabelle," replied the old woman. "She was my sister—a fine figure skater she was too! But that was long ago. She's dead now—been dead and buried for 60 years. She was just about your age when she died."

"What!" cried Heather. "She's dead? But that's impossible! How did it happen?"

"She fell through the ice by the birch trees on Mill Pond," said the woman. "It's 60 years ago today that she disappeared."

Heather stood there for a minute or two, as if her feet were glued to the floor. Then she turned around, sped through the door, and ran back to her house as fast as her legs could carry her.

Heather never told anyone about what happened that day. Life quickly went back to normal. For the rest of that winter she skated nearly every day. She performed the difficult twirls and jumps that Anabelle had taught her—though she was always very careful to make sure the ice was safe to skate on.

And once, when she was alone on the frozen pond, Heather thought she heard the *scrape, scrape* of invisible blades on ice, followed by a soft *whoosh* of air as if someone had just glided by.

Flashlight Fun

Turn out the lights! It's time for flashlight fun.

Shadow Puppets

Trace the ghost on the opposite page onto a piece of cardboard. Cut it out. Cut out holes for the eyes and mouth too. Tape a craft stick to the bottom of your figure.

In a very dark room, shine a flashlight against a wall. Hold the puppet by the stick and move it across the beam of light.

If you wish, create a cast of scary characters and put on a puppet show for your friends.

Haunted Howls

Tickle your funny bone with these spooky jokes.

How can you tell if a house is haunted?
The windows are shuddering.

What does a ghost keep in its stable?
Night-MARES.

What do ghosts like to play with instead
of Frisbees?
BOO-merangs.

What was the monster's vision?
20-20-20-20-20-20.

Why was the skeleton a coward?
He had no guts.

When is it bad luck to have a black cat follow you?
When you're a mouse.

What kind of a mistake does a ghost make?
A boo-boo.

More Flashlight Fun

Jack-O'-Lantern Flashlight

Trace the jack-o'-lantern face on the opposite page onto a brown paper lunch bag. Cut out openings for its eyes, nose, and mouth. Place the bag over a flashlight. Wind rubber bands around the bottom of the bag to hold it in place. Turn on the flashlight for a scary surprise.

What a Scream!

Here are some more jokes about ghosts and ghouls and other things that go bump in the night.

Why did the police officer arrest the ghost?
He didn't have a haunting license.

What kind of food does a ghoul eat?
GHOUL-ash.

What did the vampire say to the house?
I want to bite your deck.

What instrument does a skeleton like to play?
The trom-BONE.

Why didn't the mummy answer the phone?
He was all tied up.

What do birds say on Halloween?
Twick or tweet.

What does a witch use to tell time?
A witch watch.

The Bat

Baseball season had just started, and Billy Meyers would have given anything for a few good hits. But each time he was up at bat, it was the same old thing. Three strikes and Billy was out.

It wasn't that Billy was that bad a player. He could always count on getting a few good hits at practice. But when it came to a game, he just couldn't cut it. It was especially bad with that bully Roger Sperry always heckling and picking on him.

One day when Billy was lending a hand at the antique shop, the kind old owner, Mr. Bradshaw, asked him why he seemed so down.

"It's baseball," answered Billy. "I can't seem to get my act together this season. And the big game is only two days away."

"I have something that might help," said Mr. Bradshaw, leading Billy to the back of the shop.

"See this bat?" he said. "It's a lucky bat. I hit my first home run with it. And I'll tell you a secret—anyone I've ever lent it to has had amazing luck too. Would you like to borrow it for the big game?"

"Would I!" exclaimed Billy, his eyes shining. As Mr. Bradshaw handed him the lucky bat, Billy noticed another bat covered in cobwebs in a far corner of the room.

"Was that yours too?" Billy asked.

Mr. Bradshaw's eyes clouded over. "That one belonged to a friend. Don't know why I keep it—maybe so no one else will ever use it."

"Was your friend a good ball player?" Billy asked.

"That he was." A faraway look crept into Mr. Bradshaw's eyes, and he began to hum a nursery-rhyme tune over and over. As Billy left the shop with his lucky bat, he heard Mr. Bradshaw singing the words to "Ring Around the Rosie."

The next day at practice, Billy surprised everybody by getting three base hits and a home run.

"How did you get so good all of a sudden?" Roger asked. "What did you do? Take special vitamins?"

"It's my new bat," replied Billy. "Well, it's not really mine," Billy corrected himself. "Mr. Bradshaw at the antique shop let me borrow it. It's a good-luck bat."

"Does he have any more?" Roger asked.

"No," replied Billy. "I mean, he *does* have another bat. But Mr. Bradshaw said it belonged to a friend of his, and no one could ever use it."

After the game, Roger made a beeline to Mr. Bradshaw's shop. As he walked toward the back, he heard Mr. Bradshaw sadly singing the words "A pocket full of posey."

What a weird old guy, Roger thought. Then he saw what he came for, picked it up, and took it to the cash register. "I'd like to buy this bat," he said.

"It's not for sale," Mr. Bradshaw said firmly. "That bat stays here."

Roger returned the bat to the back of the shop and carefully placed it beneath the back window.

"We'll see if it stays here or not," he muttered. Then he quietly slipped out of the shop.

The next day at the big game all the players showed up, except Roger. *Roger never misses a game,* Billy thought. *I wonder where he is.*

But soon Billy was hitting so well that he forgot all about Roger.

On his way home, Billy stopped by Mr. Bradshaw's to return the lucky bat. Before he could even thank him, Mr. Bradshaw said, "You'll never guess what happened last night."

"What?" Billy asked.

"Someone stole my other bat," he said. "Just opened the back window, reached in, and grabbed it." Mr. Bradshaw rubbed his chin thoughtfully. "I don't know why anyone would want it, though. The thing's downright unlucky. My friend used it only once and never got a hit off it. What's worse, he died in a fire later that same night."

"That's too bad," Billy replied.

"That bat sure got popular all of a sudden," Mr. Bradshaw continued. "Roger Sperry wanted to buy it only yesterday." Just then Billy remembered that Roger hadn't been at the game, and a shiver ran down his spine.

Billy rushed out of the shop and hurried toward Roger's house. On his way, Jimmy Blake, a teammate, caught up with him.

"Did you hear the news?" Jimmy asked. "The Sperry's garage burned to the ground. The smoke even damaged the house. Roger has to spend all of next week with his grandmother."

They reached Roger's house, and Jimmy pointed to a pile of charred rubble. "See," said Jimmy. "The firefighters said it was a real close call."

Billy walked closer. The handle of the baseball bat jutted out from the middle of the blackened heap.

As he walked away, Billy could have sworn he heard an eerie voice singing "Ashes, ashes, all fall down."

The Floating Skull

Here is a fun trick to play on a friend.

Draw a skull on a sheet of white paper and color it black, but leave the eyes, nose, and mouth openings white. Have a friend stare at the drawing for a full minute. Then tell your friend to stare at a dark-colored wall. Your friend will see a white skull, not black. How spooky!

Try coloring the skull different colors. A red skull will turn green; a blue skull will turn orange; and a yellow skull will turn purple.

Don't Go In!

Up a steep, dark hill
Walked a boy named Jack.
He walked and he walked
'Till he came to a shack.

It had several broken windows,
And a rusty roof of tin.
And the wind whispered gravely,
"DON'T GO IN!"

But Jack was cold and tired,
So he walked on through the gate.
"RUN AWAY!" the wind was whistling,
"Before it's too late!"

Jack was on the steps now—
Right before the door.
"DON'T GO IN! DON'T GO IN!"
The wind began to roar.

Jack's hand was on the latch,
And he stepped inside.
"GO AWAY!" the wind was screeching.
"RUN AWAY AND HIDE!"

No one really knows
What was waiting in that shack.
But now the wind moans sadly,
"JACK IS NEVER COMING BACK!"